My Granny Went to Market
A Round-the-World Counting Rhyme

Written by Stella Blackstone
Illustrated by Christopher Corr

Barefoot Books
Step inside a story

My granny went to market
to buy a flying carpet.

She bought the flying carpet
from a man in Istanbul.
It was trimmed with yellow tassels,
and made of knotted wool.

Next she went to Thailand
and flew down from the sky
to buy herself two temple cats,
Puyin and Puchai. *

*"Puyin" means "little girl" and "Puchai" means "little boy"

Then she headed westwards
to the land of Mexico;
she bought three fierce and funny masks,
one pink, one blue, one yellow.

The flying carpet seemed to know
exactly where to take her;
they went to China next,
to buy four lanterns made of paper.*

*the symbol on the lanterns means "double happiness"

"To Switzerland!" cried Granny
as the carpet turned around.
She bought five cowbells there,
that made a funny clanking sound.

"Now Africa!" sang Granny,
"We must wake the morning sun!"
So they shimmied south to Kenya
where she bought six booming drums.

Next they headed northwards,
past the homes of mountain trolls,
to stop a while in Russia
for seven nesting dolls.

"Australia," Granny ordered,
"Take me down to Alice Springs.
I want eight buzzing boomerangs
that fly back without wings."

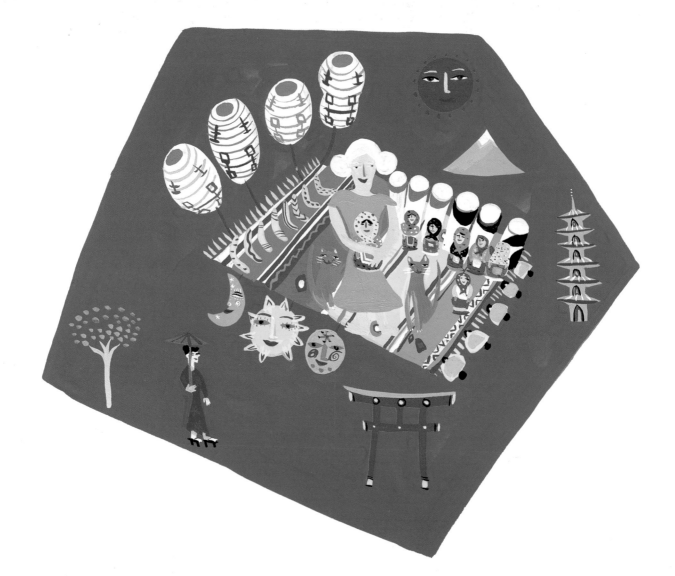

Then Granny sighed, "I've bought so much,
but nothing Japanese!"
In Tokyo she found nine kites
that fluttered in the breeze.

But best of all, she met me
in the mountains of Peru,
where she gave me ten black llamas
and a magic carpet too!

And I flew away to . . .

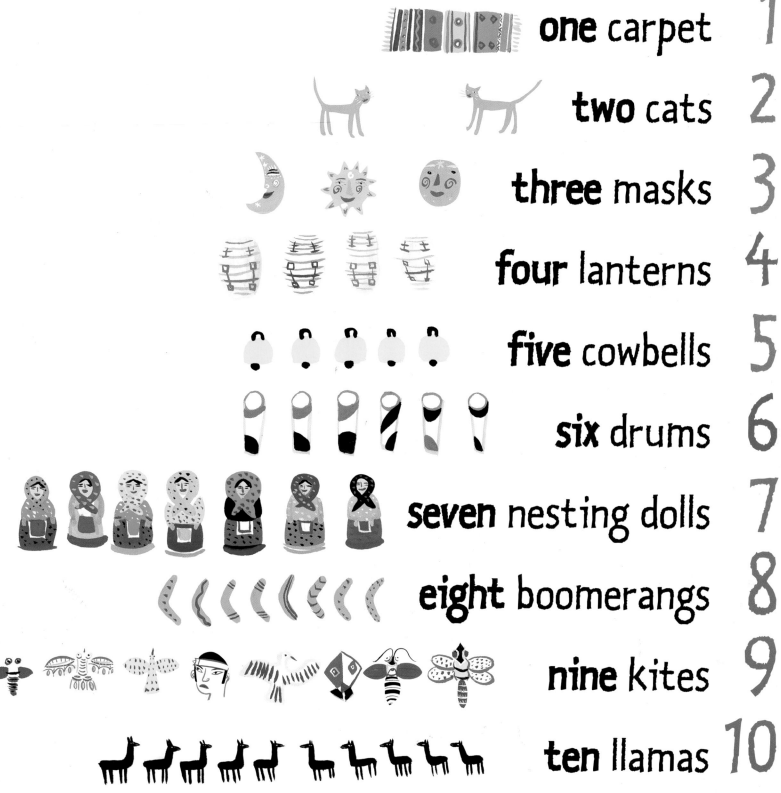

one carpet 1

two cats 2

three masks 3

four lanterns 4

five cowbells 5

six drums 6

seven nesting dolls 7

eight boomerangs 8

nine kites 9

ten llamas 10

For Felix — S. B.
For Eva Sugrue, my grandmother — C. C.

Barefoot Books
2067 Massachusetts Ave
Cambridge, MA 02140

Barefoot Books
294 Banbury Road
Oxford, OX2 7ED

Graphic design by Louise Millar
Reproduction by Grafiscan, Verona
Printed in China on 100% acid-free paper
This book was typeset in Kosmik
The illustrations were prepared in gouache on Fabriano paper

Hardback ISBN 978-1-84148-792-2
Paperback ISBN 978-1-90523-662-6

British Cataloguing-in-Publication Data:
a catalogue record for this book is available from the British Library
Library of Congress Cataloging-in-Publication Data
is available under LCCN 2004017394

3 5 7 9 8 6 4